ZEA GLOVER

STRAWBERRY CARAMEL MURDER

A Sweet Slice of Suspense
(2024 Deserts CookBook)

Copyright © 2024 by Zea Glover

All rights reserved. No part of this publication may be reproduced, stored or transmitted in any form or by any means, electronic, mechanical, photocopying, recording, scanning, or otherwise without written permission from the publisher. It is illegal to copy this book, post it to a website, or distribute it by any other means without permission.

First edition

This book was professionally typeset on Reedsy. Find out more at reedsy.com

Contents

Chapter 1	1
Chapter 2	4
Chapter 3	6
Chapter 4	9
Chapter 5	12
Chapter 6	15
Chapter 7	18
Chapter 8	20
Chapter 9	23
Chapter 10	26
Chapter 11	29
Chapter 12	32
Chapter 13	37

Chapter 1

"Who's Monica McCall?" Anabel inquired as she glanced at the newspaper clipping Bitsie had just pinned on the small bulletin board near the bakery fridge.

"She's a local food blogger, also does articles for the Fayetteville paper occasionally. Remember her glowing review of us?" Bitsie responded.

"Yeah, she was really enthusiastic about our strawberry caramel cupcakes."

"Exactly. Almost embarrassingly so," Bitsie chuckled.

"'Bitsie's Bakeshop offers the best cupcakes I've ever tasted,'" Anabel read aloud.

"Keep going," urged Bitsie.

"'A mouthful of heaven!'"

"Go on."

"'Once I'd tasted one of Bitsie's cupcakes, I knew I was ready to die a happy woman—'"

"I thought that was a bit much," Bitsie interjected. "Considering our history with murders, not the wisest choice of words. But they are good, aren't they?" Bitsie spoke with a mouthful of cupcake. "No wonder this flavor is our best-seller. Genius combination, really."

Anabel shrugged off the compliment, feeling a bit embarrassed.

"I wish the article mentioned you," Bitsie continued. "I hate taking credit where it's not due."

Anabel changed the subject quickly. "Did you hear about that guy attacking women with scissors in the grocery store parking lot last night?"

Bitsie hadn't, but it didn't surprise her. The recent incidents were alarming for the usually peaceful Little Creek.

"Did the woman get a good look at the guy?" Bitsie inquired.

"No, unfortunately," Anabel replied. "My cousin works there. I hope they catch him soon."

"I could use more strawberry caramels out there," Hector chimed in, joining the conversation.

Meanwhile, Nick entered, asking, "Who's going to seriously injure someone?"

Bitsie explained about the scissor-wielding assailant, recounting the recent incidents.

Nick frowned. "Why does someone do something like that?"

No one had an answer. Bitsie, however, didn't want to dwell on such dark topics in the bakery.

"Anyway," said Bitsie, changing the subject, "I'll be out tomorrow."

"Doing something fun?" Anabel asked.

"Not really. Dentist appointment," Bitsie replied. "But I've asked Monica McCall to swing by for some cupcakes as a thank you."

"Isn't that like a bribe?" joked Nick.

"A payment, perhaps," Bitsie retorted, tossing a rag at him.

The conversation shifted to dinner plans until Nick brought up meeting his mother, leaving Bitsie feeling uneasy about the age difference between them.

The next day, Bitsie was late for her dental appointment, only to find it canceled due to a scare involving the scissor-wielding attacker. Later, when Monica's husband called the bakery, worried about her whereabouts, Bitsie sensed something was amiss.

Chapter 2

Bitsie dialed Monica McCall's cellphone number early the next morning, feeling restless after a night of poor sleep. She tried to rationalize her worry, considering various scenarios like a rough patch in Monica and Dale's relationship or simple delays in Monica's errands. Despite her attempts to calm herself, Bitsie couldn't shake off the concern entirely.

When Monica didn't pick up, Bitsie tried the number Dale had provided, reaching him immediately. Concerned, she inquired about Monica's whereabouts, to which Dale responded with trembling uncertainty, admitting he hadn't heard from her either. Bitsie probed gently about any possible conflicts or signs of distress from Monica but found nothing conclusive.

With growing worry, Dale revealed Monica's last known whereabouts before her disappearance, prompting Bitsie to suggest reporting her missing. Dale confirmed he had already contacted the authorities and was heading to the police station. Bitsie ended the call, pondering Dale's demeanor and the unsettling possibility of foul play.

Feeling compelled to take action, Bitsie resolved to search for Monica herself. Gathering photos from Monica's blog, she prepared to canvass local businesses for information. Despite her reluctance to bother Dale further, Bitsie reached out to Anabel from the bakery, eventually getting a description of Monica's vehicle from Nick.

Armed with information, Bitsie scoured the town, encountering vague leads and speculation about Monica's disappearance. A chance encounter at the grocery store led her to Katie, a friend of Monica's, who disclosed Monica's distress over her mother's involvement in a suspected scam. Armed with this new information, Bitsie's determination to find Monica intensified, despite the looming dinner engagement with Nick's mother.

As she pursued leads and distributed missing person fliers, Bitsie grappled with the unsettling truth that Monica's vanishing could be more sinister than initially thought. Each encounter and revelation pushed her closer to unraveling the mystery behind Monica's disappearance, even as she juggled personal anxieties and obligations.

Chapter 3

Bitsie sauntered into the bakery nearly at noon, feeling the weight of the impending conversation. Rather than diving into her baking tasks, she made a beeline for her office, closing the door behind her. There was a pressing matter she needed to discuss with someone.

That someone happened to be Jane Barton. Katie, a friend of Monica, had a hunch that the local figure involved in the potential scam was a female dentist. With only two dentists in Little Creek, and one being a woman, Dr. Barton seemed to fit

CHAPTER 3

the bill.

Bitsie dialed Jane Barton's office number.

"Could you please ask Dr. Barton to call me back?" she requested the receptionist. "It's not dental-related; it's personal."

"Sure, I'll relay the message," the receptionist responded.

It wasn't until mid-afternoon that Jane returned Bitsie's call, initially showing annoyance until Bitsie mentioned her interest in Jane's recent investment opportunity. Jane agreed to meet at the bakery after her last patient, clearly eager about the discussion.

As the day dragged on, Bitsie couldn't shake her unease. She mulled over whether Jane was complicit in the scheme or simply unaware. Regardless, she needed to follow this lead, despite doubts it would uncover Monica's whereabouts.

Anabel interrupted Bitsie's thoughts, mentioning the recent news about a security camera footage of the elusive scissor creep. Bitsie had watched it but couldn't make out the culprit's identity.

The looming evening plans added to Bitsie's anxiety. Nick, oblivious to her turmoil, cheerfully inquired about their dinner date, mentioning his anticipation for trying Russian cuisine.

Bitsie forced a smile, inwardly dreading the evening. Her attire remained undecided, wanting to strike a balance between effort and nonchalance.

Nick caught her mishap in filling cupcakes, a reflection of her distracted state. Jane's arrival at 4:15, brimming with excitement, only heightened Bitsie's apprehension.

Their conversation delved into Jane's investment, revealing a dubious scheme masked as an opportunity. Despite Jane's fervor, Bitsie couldn't ignore the red flags in the glossy brochures and dubious explanations.

Bitsie's probing exposed the scheme's flaws, much to Jane's indignation. The encounter left Bitsie shaken, realizing Jane was ensnared in a scam she couldn't see through.

With a heavy heart, Bitsie resolved to take action, even as she faced Nick's obliviousness and the impending meeting with his critical mother.

She scrambled to prepare, juggling her cat's needs, attire selection, and a touch of makeup to meet Nick's mother. Despite her efforts, doubts lingered as she braced for potential disapproval.

Nick's arrival prompted a rush to the restaurant, where Bitsie fretted over potential scrutiny from his punctual mother.

In transit, she briefed Stan on her findings and plans for further investigation, arranging a breakfast meeting for the following day.

As Stan cautioned her to be careful, Bitsie assured him of her caution, aware of the risks but determined to uncover the truth behind the scam that ensnared Jane Barton and potentially Monica's mother.

Chapter 4

"I'm thinking of going for the Pelmeni," Nick declared, sliding his menu back onto the table. "It's surprising we haven't been here before."

Bitsie glanced around the softly lit restaurant, nestled on the ground floor of an ancient Victorian brick building in Fayetteville's historic downtown. The ambiance was tasteful, with crisp white tablecloths and delicate blown-glass light fixtures casting a flattering glow. It could have been romantic, if not for the presence of Sybil Konrad, the mother of the man she loved, seated across from her.

"I'm not sure about you, Nick," Sybil remarked, "but I prefer to see what I'm eating. Don't you agree, Bitsie?"

Bitsie gritted her teeth at the 'older generation' remark but managed a forced laugh. She opted for the Olivier salad, feigning interest, while inwardly fuming at Sybil's thinly veiled jabs.

Their conversation meandered through various topics, including Nick's aunt Cynthia's health, until Sybil abruptly shifted gears.

"I heard about a missing woman in Little Creek," Sybil mentioned, spearing a forkful of Veal Orlov.

Nick confirmed the news, mentioning Anabel's encounter

with the woman. The dialogue then veered into playful teasing from Sybil about Nick's romantic prospects with another woman, leaving Bitsie feeling uncomfortable and out of place.

As the evening wore on, Bitsie's discomfort grew, exacerbated by Sybil's not-so-subtle remarks about age, relationships, and societal expectations. She found solace in excusing herself to the restroom, hoping to escape the awkwardness for a moment.

Upon returning, Bitsie overheard a conversation at a nearby table, catching snippets of gossip about an affair and financial woes. It piqued her curiosity but also served as a reminder of the complexities hidden beneath seemingly ordinary lives.

Back at the table, the discomfort lingered, exacerbated by Sybil's casual remarks about diets and appearances. Bitsie struggled to maintain her composure, increasingly aware of the gaping divide between herself and Nick's family.

Later, in the privacy of Nick's car, Bitsie tentatively broached her feelings of unease, only to be met with assurances from Nick that his mother adored her. However, Bitsie couldn't shake the sense of being judged and found herself questioning the dynamics at play.

The next morning, Bitsie sought refuge in familiar company, meeting her brother Stan and his wife Liz for breakfast. Over the meal, she recounted her encounter with Jane Barton and her suspicions about InstaWealth365, seeking advice on how to proceed.

Stan's pragmatic response tempered Bitsie's fervor, reminding her of the challenges in combating such scams. Liz echoed his sentiments, highlighting the reluctance of victims to acknowledge their folly.

Bitsie's mind raced with possibilities, fueled by Dale's revelations about Monica's involvement with InstaWealth365 and her efforts to expose its deceit. She contemplated the risks and uncertainties, grappling with the weight of Monica's disappearance and the tangled web of deceit surrounding it.

As she delved deeper into the mystery, Bitsie confronted the unsettling truth that those closest to her might harbor secrets darker than she could have imagined. Yet, fueled by determination and a sense of justice, she resolved to uncover the truth, whatever the cost.

Chapter 5

"Hey, how did it go meeting Nick's mom?" Liz, Bitsie's sister-in-law, inquired as she glanced around the bakery kitchen nostalgically. "Sometimes I miss this place. Retirement feels a bit odd. Waking up in the morning with no set destination. I do miss having somewhere to be every day."

Bitsie, busy preparing fillings for the next day's raspberry ripple cupcakes, nodded. "You thinking of coming in part-time?"

Liz chuckled. "I don't know about that, but if you ever need a stand-in, I'm here."

Bitsie seized the opportunity. "Could you cover for me tomorrow?"

"Hot date?" Liz teased.

Bitsie hesitated. Confiding her plans to snoop around for information about Olga Schmidt and Jason Jameson was risky. "Not exactly," she replied evasively.

Liz raised an eyebrow. "Something related to Monica McCall's disappearance, I bet. You should tell someone, you know."

"Alright, I'll spill," Bitsie relented.

But before she could dive into the topic, Liz redirected the conversation. "So, Nick's mom… how'd it go?"

CHAPTER 5

Bitsie sighed. "Total disaster. She can't stand me, but Nick is oblivious."

Liz shook her head knowingly. "Typical. What did she say?"

Bitsie recounted the jabs about her age and insinuations about Nick and Anabel having children. "And Nick didn't find any of it inappropriate."

"Figures," Liz muttered.

Changing the subject, Bitsie mentioned her plan to attend an InstaWealth365 meeting, suspecting a link to Monica's disappearance. Liz expressed concern about Bitsie's trust in Dale, Monica's husband.

Later, Bitsie made missing-person fliers and researched Olga and Jason's homes. Her investigation led her to a possible sighting of Monica's car near the Jameson farm.

Upon reaching the location, she cautiously explored, uncovering clues but feeling increasingly uneasy. As the weather turned, she retreated, deciding to investigate the Jameson's residence next.

Chapter 6

After forty minutes, Bitsie found herself in Fayetteville. Since it was already past lunchtime, she decided to grab a hamburger before continuing her surveillance of the Jamesons. Just as she received her order, a text from Dale popped up on her phone.

"Monica left me," it read.

"Left you?" Bitsie texted back, puzzled.

"She finally contacted me last night. She's left me for another man," Dale replied.

Bitsie was torn between sympathy and skepticism. Part of her wanted to offer condolences, while the other part questioned the validity of Dale's claims. She quickly dialed Dale's number, hoping for some clarity amidst the confusion.

"Hi Bitsie," Dale answered, launching into an apology before she could get a word in. He admitted to deceiving her about his marriage and expressed regret over Monica's departure. He confessed that their marriage had been on shaky ground for a while, so Monica's decision didn't come as a complete shock. Despite his disappointment, Dale accepted Monica's choice and claimed he wouldn't stand in her way.

Bitsie couldn't shake the feeling that Dale wasn't being entirely truthful. Nevertheless, she inquired further about

Monica's departure.

"Monica called you last night?" Bitsie probed.

"Yes," Dale responded hurriedly, anticipating the question. "She didn't text."

Bitsie found Dale's explanation dubious. Why would he suddenly fabricate this story days after Monica had vanished?

"Did she mention where she went?" Bitsie pressed.

"No, just asked me not to look for her," Dale replied.

"So, divorce is on the horizon?" Bitsie asked.

"Yeah, looks like it," Dale confirmed.

The conversation left Bitsie unsettled. It seemed like an odd way to end a marriage. Suppressing her suspicions, she ended the call and left with her burger, pondering the perplexing situation.

Later, she called her brother Stan to discuss the latest developments. They speculated on Dale's possible involvement and the likelihood of police intervention. Despite uncertainty, they agreed that further investigation was necessary.

As she drove towards the Jameson residence, roadwork diverted her path. Frustrated by the delay, she redirected her navigation to the Schmidt home. Despite lacking a clear objective, she felt compelled to continue her inquiry.

The Schmidt residence was ostentatious, resembling something out of a mobster's imagination. Bitsie observed from afar, feeling out of place. Just as she was about to leave, a solemn teenager on a bike exited the property, igniting Bitsie's curiosity.

Was it Seth? Bitsie couldn't be sure, but his demeanor hinted at a troubled relationship with his mother, Olga. The thought infuriated her, fueling her determination to uncover the truth.

Returning home, Bitsie indulged in chocolate ice cream, her mind consumed by thoughts of Monica's disappearance.

The next day, as Bitsie tended to her bakery, Stan delivered alarming news: Dale had vanished. Shocked by the revelation, Bitsie struggled to comprehend the situation. Stan advised caution, emphasizing the gravity of Dale's disappearance.

Refusing to accept the worst, Bitsie resolved to continue her investigation. She contacted Monica's mother, Gwen, seeking insight into her daughter's disappearance.

With Katie's assistance, Bitsie located Gwen at a retirement home, described as a boisterous redhead. Eager to learn more, Bitsie hurried to meet her, hoping to uncover clues that would lead to Monica's whereabouts.

Chapter 7

Gwen kept up a lively chatter with herself, unaffected by the elderly woman sitting next to her who seemed lost in thought. It was unclear whether the woman was genuinely absent-minded or merely pretending. Gwen seemed perfectly content in her own world, needing no encouragement.

Bitsie, unsure how to approach Gwen directly, retreated from the common room to text Nick's grandfather, Roscoe, for assistance. Despite Roscoe's occasional negligence with his phone, luck was on her side this time. Within moments of sending the text, Roscoe called back. Bitsie stepped aside to take the call, not worried about Gwen overhearing amidst her continuous chatter.

It struck Bitsie as odd that Gwen could be so cheerful despite the recent ordeal of her daughter's apparent kidnapping and potential murder. Nevertheless, she quickly explained her presence at Shady Grove to Roscoe and what help she needed. Roscoe soon joined them in the common room, blending in with the surroundings.

After a brief wait, Bitsie entered the room and greeted Roscoe warmly, diverting attention away from Gwen's ongoing monologue about a missing casserole dish. Betty, the elderly woman, clarified that Gwen wasn't her daughter but her sister's child, a fact Gwen seemed oblivious to.

Attempting to engage Gwen, Bitsie pretended familiarity and suggested she might be Monica's mother. Gwen didn't seem to recall meeting Bitsie, but their conversation shifted to Monica's whereabouts, revealing that she had left her husband, much to Bitsie's surprise.

As the discussion unfolded, Bitsie found herself entangled in a web of half-truths and lies, unsure of Monica's true intentions. Despite Gwen's insistence on secrecy, Bitsie and Roscoe expressed relief at knowing Monica was safe, albeit perplexed by her actions.

Bitsie seized the opportunity to inquire about a supposed investment opportunity Gwen had mentioned, subtly probing for information. Gwen, initially skeptical, eventually invited Bitsie to an investor's meeting that evening, offering an opportunity for Bitsie to learn more about InstaWealth365.

Eager to unravel the mystery surrounding Monica's disappearance, Bitsie enthusiastically accepted the invitation, hoping to glean vital clues at the exclusive meeting.

Chapter 8

Gwen had called it the "Top Producer's Meeting," surprising Bitsie with its location at Olga Jameson's house. It seemed Olga's "investors" were likely impressed by opulent features like gold-plated bathroom fixtures and black marble porticos. This setting served as a psychological tactic, making Olga and Jason's targets more susceptible to the idea of living in luxurious splendor through investments in InstaWealth365.

Anxious, Bitsie clutched her tote bag's handle as she left Shady Grove with Gwen, making a pit stop at the bathroom to discreetly inform Nick and Liz of her whereabouts. She chose not to involve Stan and advised Liz to keep him in the dark, revealing only what was necessary.

CHAPTER 8

During the journey, Bitsie learned the meaning of "vetted" – she was expected to bring a stack of money for a guided visualization exercise. Despite Gwen's assurance that investing wasn't mandatory, the pressure was palpable.

Upon arrival, Bitsie questioned the necessity of withdrawing personal cash for the visualization, but Gwen insisted it enhanced the experience. To Bitsie, it seemed like a test of trust and financial capability.

As they reached Olga's house, Gwen shared rumors about an affair between Olga and Jason, allegedly spread by Monica. However, Bitsie doubted Monica as the source, considering it might just be baseless gossip. She resolved to keep an eye out for evidence supporting or refuting the claim, though its relevance to Monica's disappearance puzzled her.

Inside Olga's lavish living room, Bitsie observed a diverse group of "power investors," mostly aged sixty-plus, defining the term as those who had invested fifty thousand or more. She was relieved not to see Jane Barton, maintaining a facade of interest despite her skepticism about InstaWealth365 being akin to a Ponzi scheme.

The meeting commenced with Jason's pep talk, followed by power investors reporting their earnings and recruits. Olga then led a wealth visualization exercise, where guests placed their money on a table and chanted affirmations. Bitsie found the ritual bizarre but maintained her composure.

After the chanting, Bitsie hesitated to invest, citing the need to consult her boyfriend. Despite Olga's pressure, she stood her ground, leaving the meeting feeling unfulfilled and convinced of Olga's dominance in the partnership with Jason.

The next morning, Bitsie woke to unsettling news of a woman believed to have jumped off a bridge, fearing it might be

Monica. Anxious and restless, she sought solace in routine, pondering over bizarre dreams and contemplating potential cupcake surprises.

A disturbing report on a teenager's hair-collecting spree and Monica's disappearance added to Bitsie's distress. Stan's updates on the situation offered little comfort, leaving Bitsie grappling with uncertainty and a lingering hope that Monica might still be alive.

Despite her resolution to stay out of the investigation, Bitsie couldn't shake the feeling of obligation towards Monica. Ignoring her initial reluctance, she embarked on a search for Dale, determined to find answers before facing another day at the bakery.

Chapter 9

Bitsie found herself inundated with tasks as soon as she arrived at the bakery. The place appeared to be twice as bustling as usual, leaving Bitsie feeling like she and Nick hadn't had any quality time together since their dinner with Sybil. Amidst her preoccupation with Monica's disappearance, she hadn't spared a thought for what Nick's mother might think of her.

By mid-afternoon, Bitsie was utterly exhausted. Seeking respite from the frenzy, she slipped into the office for a brief reprieve, accompanied only by Nick as Hector and Anabel, the morning bakers, had already left. With no customers in sight for the moment, Nick trailed after her.

"I feel like I haven't really seen you in days, other than in passing," Nick remarked.

Bitsie nodded in agreement, realizing she had been keeping too much from Nick. Gathering her courage, she decided to confess what she'd been occupying herself with instead of spending time with him.

"Wow," Nick exclaimed once Bitsie had finished recounting her story. "I really wish you wouldn't embark on these solo escapades."

Bitsie explained it wasn't intentional, but she did have a

few loose ends to tie up. She proposed involving Nick in her investigative ventures, hoping he wouldn't fret if she promised to include him.

"There are a couple of places I want to check out," Bitsie admitted. "Though they might lead nowhere. If I can get Liz to cover closing tonight, would you be up for some sleuthing with me?"

"What's your plan?" Nick inquired.

"I've never driven past the Jameson's place, and I want to revisit that farm. But it's too dark for that tonight. I have this nagging feeling something's amiss there, especially after what Fred from Speedy Pete's told me about Monica's car possibly being parked nearby on the day she disappeared."

"Alright," Nick agreed. "I'll join you if you can arrange coverage with Liz, but I won't condone breaking and entering."

After securing Liz's agreement to cover for them, Nick and Bitsie set off for Fayetteville to drive by the Jameson residence. However, their plans hit a snag as Bitsie's oil light illuminated just as they approached the outskirts of Fayetteville.

CHAPTER 9

"Is this thing leaking oil again?" Bitsie lamented rhetorically, recalling her frequent visits to the mechanic.

"We should get some before proceeding," Nick suggested as they spotted a store ahead.

While waiting in line at checkout, Bitsie abruptly directed Nick to check stand five without explanation, insisting he act natural for the time being.

As they observed a woman ahead of them making purchases, Bitsie declared they must follow her once they left the store, disregarding the urgency of replenishing the oil.

The woman, later identified as Hannah Jameson, led them to unexpected places, including a motel in a run-down area where she met with someone for an extended period.

Determined to uncover the truth, Bitsie persuaded Nick to return the next morning before work to investigate further.

The following day, Bitsie's suspicions were heightened by a disturbing news report about another person found near County Road 48 bridge, mirroring Monica's disappearance.

Certain that one of the victims was Dale, she contacted Stan, hoping for more information.

Later, she and Nick revisited the motel, only to find the room vacated and being cleaned. Using a white lie to gain access, Bitsie sifted through the trash, finding evidence linking Hannah Jameson to the room's occupant.

Despite Nick's skepticism, Bitsie felt reassured by their findings, convinced that Monica was still alive, and Hannah was aiding her.

Chapter 10

Bitsie and Nick returned to the bakery just in time to take over from Anabel and Hector. Nick relieved Anabel at the front, while Bitsie got to work frosting a fresh batch of banana cream cupcakes that Hector had baked earlier.

As she worked, Bitsie mulled over her next steps. Discovering hair dye and a disposable phone package in a motel trashcan was one thing, but going to the police and claiming that the presumed-dead Monica was alive and hiding somewhere was another. Despite her conviction that Monica had been in that room, she couldn't fathom why. Could it be that Monica's disappearance was a ruse? Was her supposed suicide staged to cover up something more sinister, like the disappearance of her husband? Bitsie found it hard to believe Monica capable of murder. There had to be another explanation for their odd behavior.

She resolved to speak with Gwen, Monica's mother, as soon as possible. Though they hadn't seen each other since attending an InstaWealth365 meeting, their last interaction had been amicable. Gwen wasn't one for discretion, but when she claimed Monica had contacted her after her disappearance, Bitsie believed her. She was certain Monica was still alive and would have reached out to her mother.

CHAPTER 10

Apart from Gwen, Bitsie wanted to interview Hannah Jameson, sensing a connection between her and Monica. However, she couldn't decipher what it might be.

Once she finished frosting the cupcakes, Bitsie retreated to the bakery office and dialed Gwen's number.

"Hello, Bitsie!" Gwen's voice was far from mourning. "Have you decided to invest?"

Ignoring Gwen's sales pitch, Bitsie got to the point. "I heard about Monica. Is she really okay? Have you heard from her?"

"Yes," Gwen confirmed. "She called last night, assuring me she's fine. Asked me not to worry."

Bitsie couldn't help but wonder if Gwen had spread this information to others. Nonetheless, she refrained from mentioning it, considering the implications for the police investigation.

"Why did she leave her car on the bridge?" Bitsie inquired.

Gwen shrugged off the question. "I don't know. She didn't tell me much."

As their conversation progressed, Bitsie sensed Gwen's sadness about Dale's apparent suicide. However, she couldn't shake her doubts about the circumstances.

After hanging up, Bitsie was interrupted by Nick, who informed her of Gregory's presence. She approached Gregory, offering assistance and learning about his missing son, Seth.

Later, she returned home to feed her cat and caught up with the news, learning about possible sightings of Dale and Monica. While having dinner with Nick, her brother Stan called with updates on the Monica McCall case.

Stan revealed shocking news about Olga Schmidt's disappearance and the discovery of bloodstains in her home. Bitsie speculated about Olga's involvement, considering her troubled relationship with her son, Seth.

After the call, Bitsie discussed the developments with Nick before continuing her own investigation, keeping her suspicions close to her chest for the time being.

Chapter 11

Once Bitsie arrived home, she swiftly powered up her laptop and settled at her kitchen table. There was a pressing need for some detective work regarding young Seth. The longer he remained missing, the more her apprehension grew. She couldn't shake off the worry about the potential dangers lurking for a kid out there. It was high time to buckle down and track down Seth Schmidt to bring him back home.

Considering Seth likely departed on his bicycle, and if it hadn't been discovered yet, he probably hadn't strayed far. Being a solitary individual, with his few close friends denying any knowledge of his whereabouts, left one plausible scenario: Seth was hiding in a familiar place, somewhere he frequented before. A sensible teenager wouldn't opt for checking into a hotel, as that would attract unwanted attention. So, Seth was likely still somewhere within Little Creek, possibly enduring a discomforting time outdoors.

Bitsie considered the homeless community camping on public land north of town but dismissed the idea of Seth seeking refuge there, as he would likely avoid contact with unfamiliar adults.

With Gregory's missing person social media page in view,

Bitsie searched for specific clues. Most photos depicted Seth on his bike, showcasing his passion for BMX trail-riding. The wooded landscapes hinted at potential hiding spots, perhaps with homemade obstacles.

Bitsie's investigation led her to the satellite view of the neighborhood, revealing a stream at the bottom of the hillside, potentially flowing into Little Creek. Armed with this information, she printed a map and retired for the night, ready to commence her search at dawn.

The next morning, without notifying anyone of her whereabouts but leaving a note detailing her plans, Bitsie embarked on her quest. She equipped herself with breakfast provisions and headed towards the Schmidt's subdivision.

Before reaching the neighborhood, she spotted a trail into the woods, waiting for the light to improve before proceeding. Her expectation was to find a concealed shelter or tent, indicative of Seth's presence.

Walking through the woods, Bitsie stumbled upon a makeshift bike jump, hinting at Seth's activities. Climbing for a better view, she misjudged her landing, twisting her ankle in the process. Stranded and without cell service, she resorted to calling for help, hoping someone would hear her.

CHAPTER 11

Amidst the forest silence, a rustling indicated a presence, and soon, Seth emerged, cautiously approaching. Bitsie, injured but determined, shared her provisions with him and revealed her intentions to bring him home.

Their conversation unfolded, unveiling Seth's troubled family dynamics and a potential connection to a mysterious incident involving his mother. As they awaited rescue, Bitsie gleaned valuable insights into Seth's predicament, realizing the complexity of the situation.

Upon rescue, Seth's emotional reunion with his father underscored the gravity of the situation. Bitsie, despite her injury, redirected their attention towards the unresolved mystery, prompting further action.

As Bitsie, now accompanied by Nick and Liz, redirected them towards the old Marson farm, her determination to uncover the truth remained steadfast, despite the physical toll.

Chapter 12

They drove in silence towards the rundown Marson property. Nick steered down the gravel drive, parked by the weathered farmhouse, and turned off the engine. "Well, here we are," he said. "I don't know what you hope to achieve by coming here."

"I need to check out the barn again," said Bitsie.

"The barn?" Nick questioned. "You plan to hike all the way out there on your injured ankle?"

"No, I plan to get a lift all the way out there."

"A lift?"

"Gregory Schmidt carried me half a mile out of the woods this morning. Didn't even break a sweat, but then you aren't quite as big as Gregory so—"

"I see what you're doing," Nick grumbled, but he got out and went around to the passenger side of the car.

Bitsie piggybacked on Nick all the way to the barn. Unlike before, when it was tightly sealed, the large door at the end of the barn was wide open. An old, rusty front-end loader was parked inside.

"Looks like someone's been digging over there," observed Nick. "I wonder why?"

He gestured to the side of the barn where a patch of dirt about

CHAPTER 12

ten feet by ten feet had been scraped and removed.

"Let's go inside," said Bitsie.

"Inside?"

"Yes. It's farm etiquette. First, you call out to the open barn door, and if no one answers, then it's acceptable to enter and look around for the farmer."

"This place is abandoned. There is no farmer," Nick pointed out.

"The principle still stands," Bitsie insisted. "Don't carry me, I'll just hop along."

She hopped through the open door without waiting for Nick's response.

"Yoo-hoo!" she called out, "Anybody home?"

There was silence. She hopped over to the closed door of a small tack room at the end of the stalls just inside the open barn door. She tried the knob. It opened.

"Come on," Bitsie said to Nick.

"Do you really think this hypothetical farmer is going to be down there?"

Inside the tack room, against the back wall, a crude stairway descended into the cellar. Bitsie hopped down it, with Nick reluctantly following. When she reached the bottom, she held onto the stone wall and surveyed the dirt-floored cellar. Light streamed in from a small, dusty window high up on the wall. This wasn't the same room she'd glimpsed during her first visit to the farm. This one contained a cot piled with mismatched bedding and a couple of rusty folding chairs.

"Look!" Bitsie exclaimed to Nick, pointing to a pile of fast food boxes and snack wrappers piled in the corner. "One of our bakery boxes!"

She hopped over to the box and picked it up. It was the same size they used for a dozen cupcakes. A few crumbs remained inside. Bitsie picked up one between her thumb and forefinger and brought it up to her nose.

"Strawberry caramel!"

"You think Monica McCall was hiding out here?" Nick asked.

"Not hiding, exactly," Bitsie paused and glanced up once more at the dusty window. "It's gone!"

"What's gone?"

"The barrel."

"What barrel?"

"Let's go up; I'll explain everything later."

Hopping back up the stairs proved too difficult, so Nick carried her out of the barn.

"Satisfied now?" he asked.

Bitsie hopped around to the side of the barn, where the barrel had been blocking the window during her first visit. It was gone, along with the large metal lid that had caused Bitsie to stub her toe last time.

"Look at those tracks," Bitsie said, pointing to the imprints left by heavy equipment in the soft earth. "Probably from that front-end loader. It looks like they lead all the way down to the pond. Can you go check?"

Nick jogged off, leaving Bitsie standing by the side of the barn. Five minutes later, he returned.

"It seems that front-end loader drove straight into the pond."

"I'm ready to go to the hospital now," Bitsie said.

"Are you sure?" Nick asked. "You don't want me to search the crawl space under the house or climb up on the roof and peek down the chimney while I'm at it?"

"No," Bitsie replied firmly. "That won't be necessary. I have all the information I need."

CHAPTER 12

On their way to the hospital, Bitsie called Stan.

"I'm just leaving the old Marson place," Bitsie told her brother. "Tell your officers they had better go and fish that body out of the pond."

"What pond?" Stan demanded. "What body?"

"I'm confident there's a deceased person in an old metal barrel, submerged in the bottom of the pond at the old Marson place. Just inform Gladwell to go out there and investigate. It shouldn't be difficult, considering Monica McCall's car was spotted nearby."

"You think someone disposed of Monica McCall in the bottom of a cow pond?"

"Not Monica."

"Not Monica? Then who?"

"I'd rather not spoil the police's sense of accomplishment. Just send a couple of officers out there, and they'll soon see the need to dredge the pond. Think about it. There are three missing persons, all with some connection to the Jameson family, the current owners of the old Marson farm."

"You better be correct, Bitsie," Stan warned. "Because if I persuade Gladwell to get a warrant and send someone out to dredge a cow pond, and there's nothing there but an empty barrel, I'll never hear the end of it."

Twenty-four hours later, there was a team at the old Marson place combing the bottom of the pond. Stan instructed Bitsie not to interfere, but once the dredging was complete, he called her.

"You were right," he said. "They just retrieved the barrel and opened it. It's hard to identify the body at this stage, but it's definitely a blond woman. I'm sorry, Bitsie. I know you were convinced Monica McCall was still alive."

"I'm still certain it's not Monica," said Bitsie. "Monica isn't currently blond. That must be Olga Schmidt, and I'm convinced Jason Jameson was involved in her demise, although he might not have had much choice."

"I have no clue what you're talking about," Stan admitted. "You can elaborate on your theory to me later. Given the condition of the body, it'll be a while before we get a positive identification. By the way, Liz wanted me to ask if you and Nick would like to come to dinner at our place this evening."

By dinner time, Stan had changed his stance about Bitsie keeping her theories to herself.

Before Liz served the first plate of chicken parmesan, Stan addressed his sister. "You were right once again, Bitsie."

"Oh, really? About what?" she asked innocently.

Stan looked sheepish. "I don't know how you figured it all out, but when they brought Jason and Hannah Jameson in for questioning, they both cracked under pressure."

"Hannah didn't have anything to do with Olga's demise, did she?" Bitsie inquired.

"No," Stan assured her. "That was all Jason's doing, though he's claiming self-defense."

"Before you continue," Bitsie said, unable to resist showing

Chapter 13

"Dale's still alive, surprisingly. I reckon they thought a staged copycat suicide would be the best way for him to vanish quickly, so he and Monica could take off wherever they went," Bitsie remarked.

"But how did Olga end up dead?" Nick inquired.

"I'm certain Jason killed her and disposed of her in the pond," Bitsie asserted, "but the exact reasons or methods, I'm not sure. That's for Stan to disclose." She turned to her brother. "How's my summary so far? Did I miss anything?"

"If Monica McCall was hiding out in a motel in Fayetteville, how did she end up there?" Stan questioned.

"I reckon it got too risky leaving Monica alone in the cellar. Perhaps Olga became more insistent on finishing Monica off, and the others feared Olga might go to the farm alone and do the job herself. Remember, Olga might not have known anyone besides Jason was aware of her involvement with Monica's disappearance. She likely thought she could kill Monica, dispose of the body, and avoid getting caught as long as she kept Jason quiet," Bitsie explained.

"So, Hannah helped Monica find a place to hide until they could fake her death?" Liz deduced.

"That's what I believe. Hannah gave Monica an untraceable

phone for communication and hair dye to change her appearance," Bitsie confirmed.

"How did you know it was Monica in that motel room?" Liz inquired.

"We followed Hannah Jameson to the hotel from the store, where we saw her buying items that didn't fit her usual profile. Junk food, for instance," Bitsie elaborated. "Hannah seems like the type to stick to organic foods. And the hair dye was another clue; Hannah wouldn't use off-the-shelf products with her expensive highlights. Plus, the pay-as-you-go cellphone is unusual for someone wealthy."

"Not unless they want untraceable calls," Stan added.

"What really convinced me it was Monica in that motel room was finding the pizza box with leftover cheese. I knew Monica was lactose intolerant," Bitsie concluded, as the table fell into a thoughtful silence.

"It's your turn, Stan," Bitsie said, eager to hear more about Olga's demise.

Stan cautioned, "Remember, everything I say stays in this room. It'll all come out during the trial, but if it leaks beforehand, it could jeopardize the case."

"Why are you singling me out?" Bitsie protested.

"Because you're the most curious," Stan replied. "Do you promise to keep it confidential?"

"I promise," Bitsie assured.

"I can't confirm every detail," Stan began, "but according to Jason Jameson—bearing in mind his potential bias—Olga summoned him to the farm the day she died. Text messages on his phone seem to support this. Jason claims Olga believed he'd killed Monica until she saw ATM footage showing Monica alive. Upset by this revelation, Olga confronted Jason at the

CHAPTER 13

farm. He alleges she pulled a gun on him, leading to a struggle where the gun went off accidentally, killing her."

"Why didn't he call the police immediately?" Liz interjected. "Wouldn't Olga's death corroborate his story?"

"It might have if Olga had been shot with her own gun, but she wasn't. The gun belonged to Jason," Stan clarified. "Olga intended to frame Jason for her murder, coercing him into drafting a confession and suicide note. However, during their altercation, Jason managed to disarm her."

"Do you believe him?" Bitsie asked.

"The evidence supports his account, except we can't ascertain if the shooting was accidental or deliberate," Stan admitted. "Ultimately, a jury will decide. But at the very least, Jason should be convicted for false imprisonment."

After a reflective pause, Nick expressed relief that the ordeal was over, prompting Bitsie to remark on Dale and Monica's safety, acknowledging her persistent worry.

The next day, Bitsie contacted Gwen, urging her to relay a message to Monica, indicating the danger was over. Later, she discovered Monica's whereabouts in Mexico and arranged for their return home.

Upon receiving Monica's call, Bitsie assured her of their safety and planned a reunion. Monica expressed gratitude, acknowledging Bitsie's crucial role in their ordeal's resolution.

As Bitsie wiped frosting from a mixer paddle, Nick approached, and they shared a tender moment, anticipating a future free of perilous adventures.

www.ingramcontent.com/pod-product-compliance
Lightning Source LLC
LaVergne TN
LVHW020447080526
838202LV00055B/5371